To the original StinkyKids, Max and Emma.

Thank you for providing such entertaining real-life material for the StinkyKids adventures.

To my husband , Mark.

Thank you for always striving to make me better.

To Greg Hardin, John Trent, Kathy Gunter, and Kelli Ritter.

Thank you for believing in my little stinkers and
providing your talents to make them come to life.

• •

Text ©2011 Menzies, Britt

StinkyKids® characters and likenesses are trademarks of and copyrighted by StinkyKids, LLC.
All rights reserved. For information about permission to reproduce selections from this book,
write to: Permissions, Raven Tree Press, a Division of Delta Systems Co., Inc., 1400 Miller Parkway,
McHenry, IL 60050 www.raventreepress.com

Menzies, Britt.

    StinkyKids® See a Full Moon / written by Britt Menzies; illustrated by Greg Hardin
    and John Trent —1 ed. — McHenry, IL ; Raven Tree Press, 2011.

    p. ; cm.

    SUMMARY: Come and enjoy this StinkyKids nighttime playdate and see if our
            little stinKers' actions become a bit too crazy. Will these friends work
            together to turn a wrong into a right and save the playdate?

ISBN 978-1-936402-03-8 hardcover

Other books in the series:
StinkyKids and the Runaway Scissors   ISBN 978-1-936402-02-1 hardcover

    Audience: Ages 10 and under.

    1. Imagination & Play — Juvenile fiction. 2. Friendship/Social Issues —
    Juvenile fiction. 3. Manners/Social Issues — Juvenile fiction. I. Illust. Hardin, Greg;
    Trent, John. II. Title.

Library of Congress Control Number: 2011923167

Printed in the USA
10 9 8 7 6 5 4 3 2 1
First Edition

Free activities for this book are available at www.raventreepress.com

made in USA

About StinkyKids®

From the creative mind of Britt Menzies, a mom who was inspired by her daughter's simple request to paint her as a ballerina, **StinkyKids** is a brand with a fun, unique, and fresh approach that teaches life lessons through its products and books featuring the 10 diverse **StinkyKids** characters. The name "**StinkyKids**" comes from the phrase "little stinkers," which Britt used to describe the innocent behavior of her two kids when they were little.

The **StinkyKids** characters are little stinkers who learn to make right choices through their childhood mistakes and who live by the motto: "Always Be A Leader Of Good." **StinkyKids** is an innovative brand that appeals to parents for the values it represents and appeals to kids because the characters are real kids getting into real mischief.

Since its inception, **StinkyKids** donates a percentage of its profits to Books, Bears and Bonnets, Inc., (www.booksbearsbonnets.org), a charity founded in honor of Britt's aunt, who died from uterine cancer. Books, Bears and Bonnets, Inc., delivers gift boxes to children and adults fighting cancer and other life-threatening illnesses.

Come and play with the StinkyKids at **www.stinkykids.com**!

Love your StinkyKids... they're so stinkin' cute!!

"Found ya, Skye!" Trey shouted. He shined his flashlight behind the berry bush at his friend. The StinkyKids were playing flashlight hide-n-seek during a nighttime playdate at Trey's house.

Skye jumped. "I didn't hear you coming, Trey!" she said.
"I was looking at the full moon...see?" Skye pointed to
the brightest and fullest moon she had ever seen.

Johnny called the other StinkyKids over to look at the moon.
"Are you sure that's not Mercury or Uranus?" he giggled.
They all shined their flashlights up to the sky. They were
enchanted by the moon's bright light.

Skye was very excited about the full moon. "Do you know full moons make you act **crazy**?" she said.

"Aaooo!" Billy howled.

"So that means we will be extra **crazy** tonight!" said Trey.

"Yeah!" all the StinkyKids yelled. They ran around the backyard like animals who just escaped from the zoo.

The cowbell hanging outside the back door rang.
"Cookies are ready!" Trey's mom called.
"Last one inside is a rotten egg!" Billy yelled.

Hannah, Trey's big sister, was inside building a
house of cards. She had worked on it all day.
She was only a few cards away from finishing it.

The other StinkyKids ran into the room.

"Let's make a pretend movie of us acting **crazy!** I'll be the movie director," Johnny said. Hannah was worried that the other kids might knock over her house of cards.

"We could play the Quiet Game," she said. But the other kids did not listen.

"Watch this!" Jen said. She twirled around the room like a ballerina, bumping into furniture.

"How about this?" Skye yelled. She showed off her amazing somersaults.

11

"Please be careful, Skye!" Hannah said. She put another card on top of her house. "You almost knocked down my beautiful house!"

But the other StinkyKids still didn't listen. They were having lots of fun acting **full moon crazy!**
Suddenly Trey yelled, "Hey Johnny, film this!" He grabbed the sides of his pants...!
Jen looked shocked. Billy and Skye got the giggles. And all the StinkyKids yelled...

All the little stinkers except Hannah laughed.

"TREY! Please stop!" Hannah said. She was embarrassed about her brother's trick. "Everyone is making me very nervous about my house of cards!"

Hannah put another card on her house.

"Okay!" Billy said. "How about...playing ball instead? Here, Trey, catch!" Billy threw a football to Trey. But Trey missed it!

"Hey kids, here's some yummy cookies...**Ow!**" Oh no! The ball hit Trey's dad in the head. "Kids, don't play ball in the house!" he said. "You can have fun, but use inside voices and settle down!"

But the StinkyKids **STILL** did not settle down. They were laughing at Johnny. Johnny was making his famous underarm noises **AND** working the pretend camera at the same time!

"That is not using inside voices!" Hannah said. She laid the last two cards on her castle. She sat back and smiled a proud and happy smile.

The StinkyKids had laughed so hard there were cookie crumbs everywhere. Skye, the chef of the StinkyKids, thought up a wonderful cookie crumb recipe on the spot!

"Jen, want to taste my cookie crumb recipe?" Skye said. She jumped up to bring Jen the bowl but...**oops!** She spilled it instead! "**SKYE!**" Hannah said. "Calm down, please!"

Johnny said, "Hannah, you are not being fun. Here is a joke to make you laugh! Why did the dog howl at the moon?"

"I don't know! Why?" all the StinkyKids yelled.

"Because he had to go to the bathhhrooom!" Johnny howled as he said the last word. All the StinkyKids howled along with him, except Hannah.

"Johnny, that joke does not even make sense!" Hannah said.

"Well, if you're going to howl, you need another full moon!"
Trey said, as he grabbed the sides of his pants and slipped in
the watery cookie crumbs!

Skye looked shocked. Billy and Jen got the giggles. But
Johnny looked worried. "Look out!" he yelled. "You're heading
straight for the...**house of cards!**"

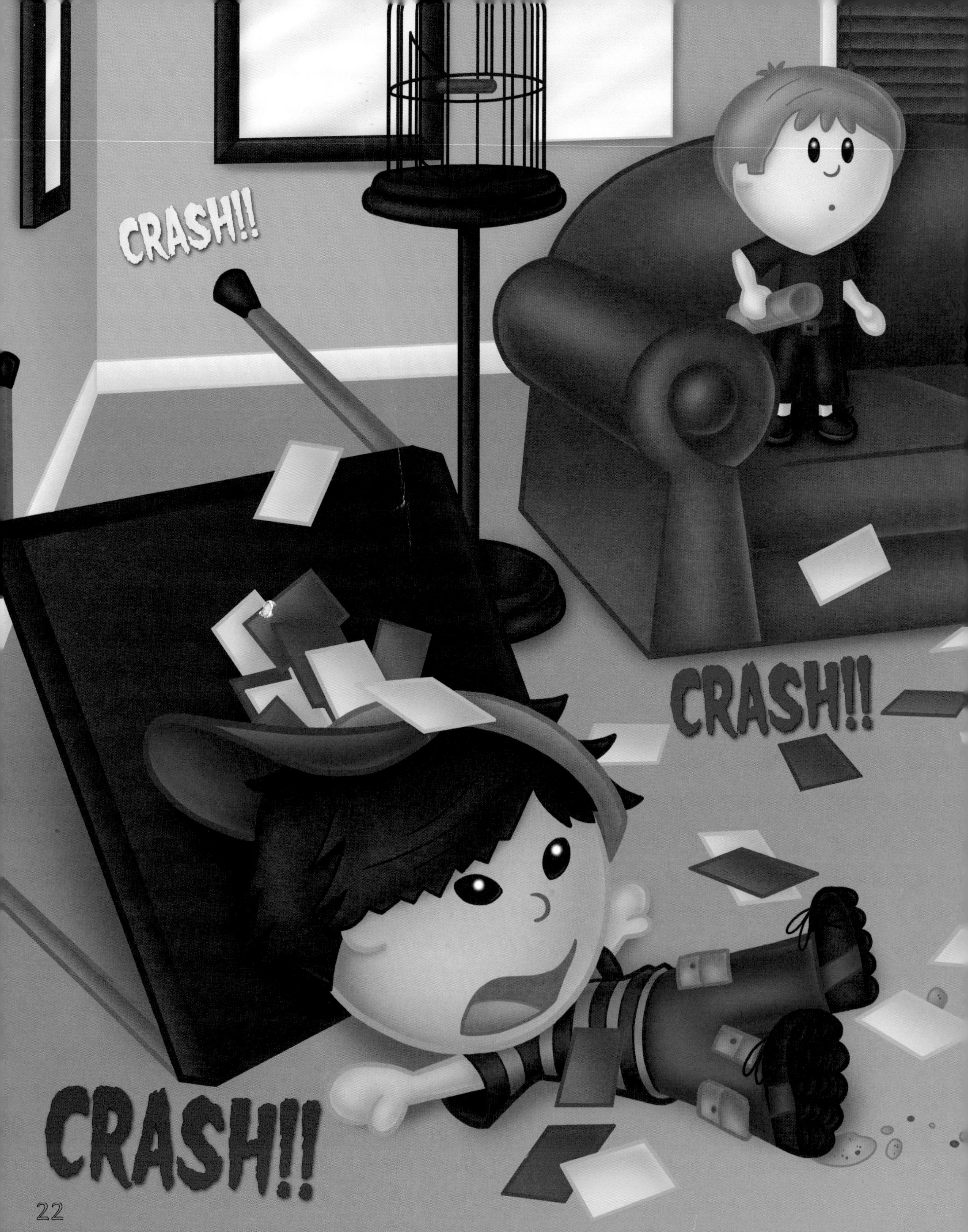
CRASH!!
CRASH!!
CRASH!!

Cards scattered all over the room. The StinkyKids
looked at their friend Hannah. Hannah was crying.
Her house of cards was ruined. The StinkyKids
knew they had taken their fun too far.

Hannah wiped a giant tear away. "I asked you to be careful around my house of cards. I worked on it all day. But you would not listen and now look..."

Jen gave Hannah a big hug. She said, "You are right, Hannah. We got too crazy. We should have listened to you. We're sorry."

"Hey everybody!" Billy said. "Let's be Leaders of Good! Let's clean up and tomorrow we'll help Hannah rebuild her house of cards."

"I'll make you a ham and cheese sandwich," said Skye. "That's my specialty."

"And I'll clean up the cookie crumb mess," Jen said.

Johnny made a silly face to make Hannah laugh. Trey did the brother-and-sister secret handshake to show Hannah he was sorry. Hannah was feeling better and did the secret handshake right back.

Trey and Hannah's dad and mom were proud that the StinkyKids had decided to be Leaders of Good. "Thanks for cleaning up, kids," they said. "And now, everyone into their sleeping bags! Let's put on a nice, **CALM** movie and we'll make some popcorn."

"We can pretend we're at a movie theater!" Hannah said.

"Yay!" the other StinkyKids said. "That will be fun!"

Everyone was quiet until a full moon appeared in the movie. "That reminds me..." Trey said. He got out of his sleeping bag. "A full moon makes you act **crazy**..."

What do YOU think happened next?

Dr. Kelli's Parent and Teacher Corner

As a mother, educator, and child/family relationship expert, I am always on the lookout for creative, fun ways to engage children. I was thrilled to meet StinkyKids' creator Britt Menzies and learn about her adorable "Leaders Of Good." StinkyKids stories involve learning through social interaction, creating many opportunities for growth in social development.

StinkyKids® See a Full Moon is a perfect story to engage children in dialogue about making good choices, respecting others, and taking responsibility for our actions. This story resonates with me personally because as we with children all know, evening playdates are especially unique. Just like the little stinkers in the story, my own kids are, as Trey put it, "even crazier" during nighttime playdates. *StinkyKids® See a Full Moon* is refreshing because it demonstrates that it is okay for children to be children. We were once just like them — exploring, learning, making lasting friendships. At the same time, the story teaches kids that sometimes fun can go too far and we need to learn to manage our behavior.

As in all of the StinkyKids books, *StinkyKids® See a Full Moon* intentionally ends with a question designed to foster ideas from children, sparking interaction between adult and child. We can learn a great deal from our children if we follow their lead and let them express themselves!

Using this Story as a Teaching Tool

It is never too early to start having conversations with children about the things we believe are important. *StinkyKids® See a Full Moon* is a great story to inspire such conversations. An important concept that is expressed in this story is for parents to help kids learn appropriate limits. Trey's parents had to set some limits with the StinkyKids during their nighttime playdate. An effective tool that I teach parents and teachers when setting limits with children involves a four-step process:

- First, start with an empathy statement. You will get more cooperation from children. An empathy statement might be "You're having so much fun with that toy" or "You are really enjoying your friends."

- Next, set the limit in a neutral tone and avoid using "no." You might say, "But it's not okay to throw balls in the house."

- Third, give one to three choices. Giving children choices after you've stated a limit will help them have a sense of control. You can say, "You can throw the ball outside, or choose to play an inside game."

- Finally, restate the limit in the same neutral tone you used before. Continuing with the example here you would say, "But the ball is not for throwing inside."

In addition, the end of this story would be a great time to discuss what we as the adults expect from our children. Let them come up with ideas for "WHAT DO YOU THINK HAPPENED NEXT?" Here are some topics you and your little stinkers can discuss:

- Do you like to play hide-n-seek? Where is your favorite place to hide?
- Have you ever seen a full moon? Describe what you saw and how it made you feel.
- Can you give some examples of outdoor fun vs. indoor fun?
- Do you think Hannah did the right thing by using her words to express how she felt? What words would you use to describe your feelings?
- How do you look when you are happy? Sad? Proud? Silly? Shocked?
- Do you have a favorite joke? Can you share your joke with me?
- How would you make a friend feel better?
- What did you notice about the parrot?
- What does it mean to "Always Be A Leader Of Good"?

Suggestions to Further Engage Children

Play is the natural language of children and, certainly, the most helpful way we have to understand a child's world. Allowing your child to have free play will help her or him to make sense of what she or he is learning and the world around them. In addition, children who engage in playtime after a story are more likely to integrate the information and enhance relationships with their parents/teachers/etc. Try some focused playtime using toys, StinkyKids dolls, and/or other fun items, to let your children express their ideas about the StinkyKids situation.

Takeaway Messages

StinkyKids helps establish and strengthen important messages such as courage, leadership, making good choices, friendship, respect, and becoming "Leaders of Good." Below is a list of takeaway messages from *StinkyKids® See a Full Moon.* Enjoy sharing these with your little stinkers!

- Keep outside fun outside — learn limits
- Always help each other (work as a team)
- Take responsibility for your actions
- Clean up your mess
- Learn from your mistakes
- Be kind and respectful to others

and...
"Always Be A Leader of Good"

Kelli B. Ritter, Ph.D.

Kelli B. Ritter, Ph.D. is the founder and president of Effective Parenting, LLC in Atlanta, Georgia, and author of *Come Play with Me!*, a guide to using play skills to enhance relationships with children. For more ideas on using play or for information on Dr. Ritter, please visit www.effectiveparentingllc.com.

Let's Learn Our Solar System

The **StinkyKids** want to help you learn the names of the planets in our solar system.

With help from a grown-up, copy* these three pages and cut them out to make your own Solar System story book!

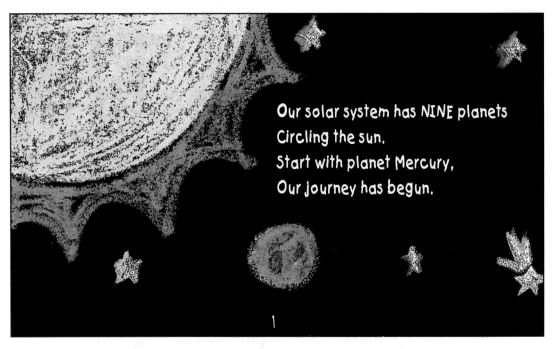

Our solar system has NINE planets
Circling the sun.
Start with planet Mercury,
Our journey has begun.

1

*These pages are also available for download on the **StinkyKids** See a Full Moon page on our website at: www.raventreepress.com.

Venus is the next in line,
A goddess full of love.
She is the **brightest** planet
In our system up above.

2

Earth the planet we call home.
A wonderful place to be.
Trees, flowers, mountains, too,
so much for us to see.

3

Planet Mars is colored Red
and fourth from the sun.
He's not as large as Jupiter
Whose size is **Number One**.

4

Next to Jupiter, we see Saturn,
with rings so **Big** and **Bright**.
Uranus is the seventh planet.
Did we pronounce it right?

5

Still further out is Neptune
Icy cold and **Blue**.
Remembered as the God of Sea,
It's really very true.

6

The **NINTH** planet is Pluto
The smallest is its fame.
Now we know our solar system.
How many can you name?

7